AF228640

Teacher

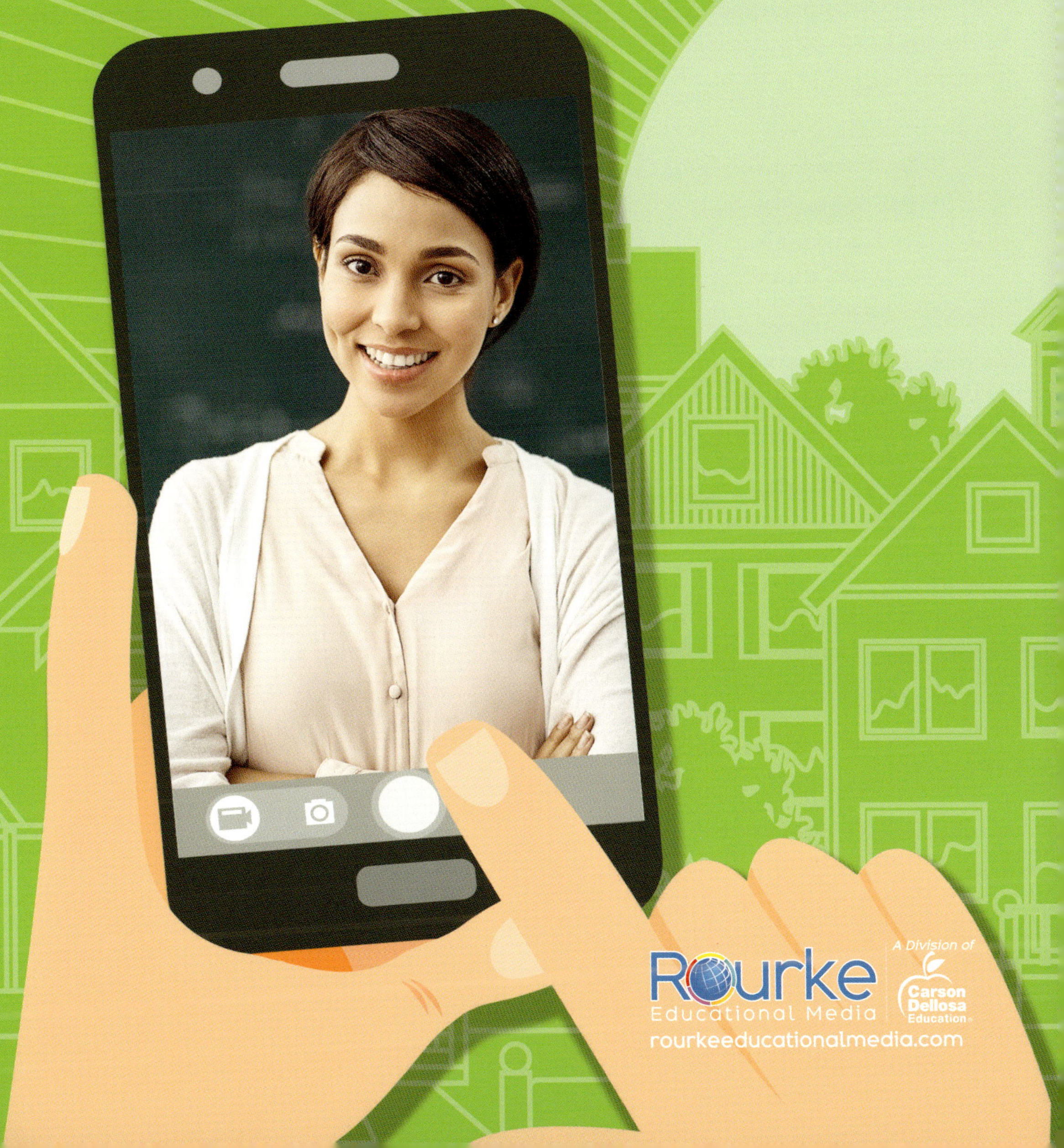

Jeff Barger

Rourke Educational Media
A Division of Carson Dellosa Education
rourkeeducationalmedia.com

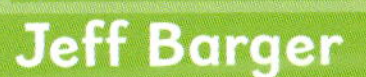

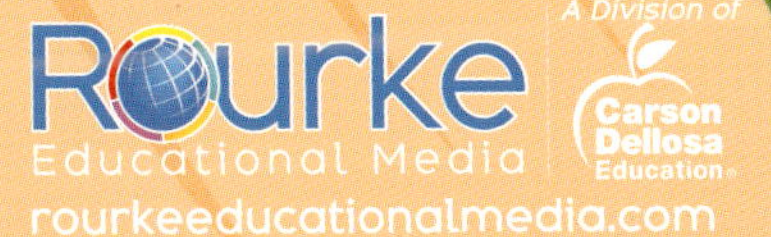

Table of Contents

Community Helpers

Community helpers are all around us. They make our lives better.

Teachers work at schools.

These helpers lead students.

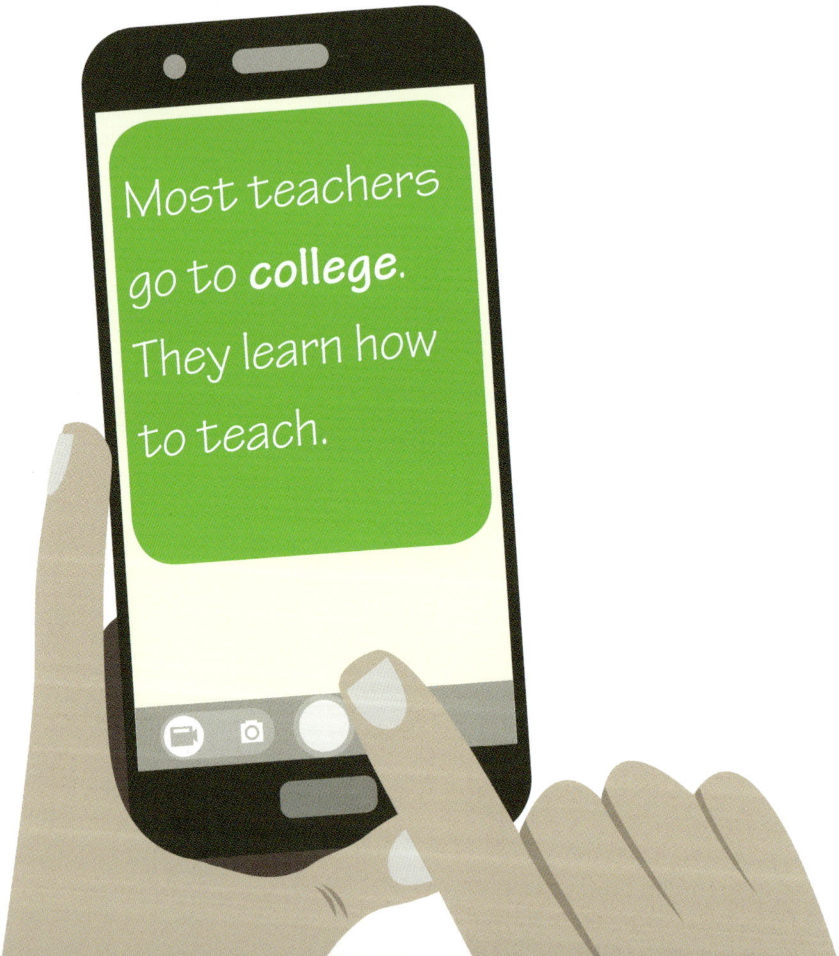

In Class

The day starts. The teacher greets students as they come in.

The bell rings.

The teacher is ready to begin.

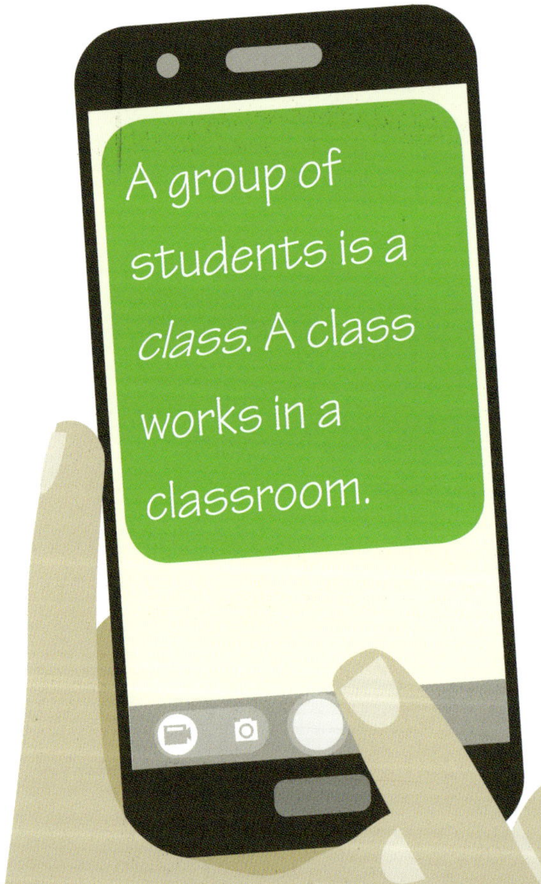

ive out people
who work
get
use
6. bike
7. dime
8. hide
9. ice
10. kite

This **lesson** is about adding.

An example is given.

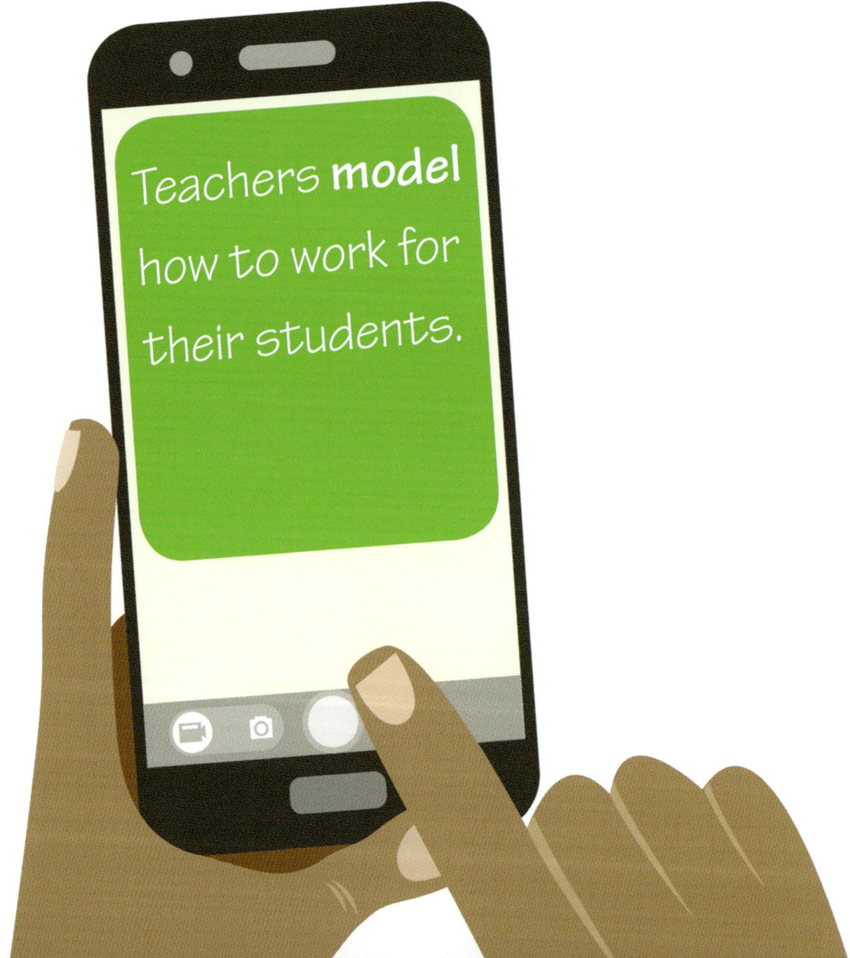

The class adds. They write.

The teacher listens as they talk.

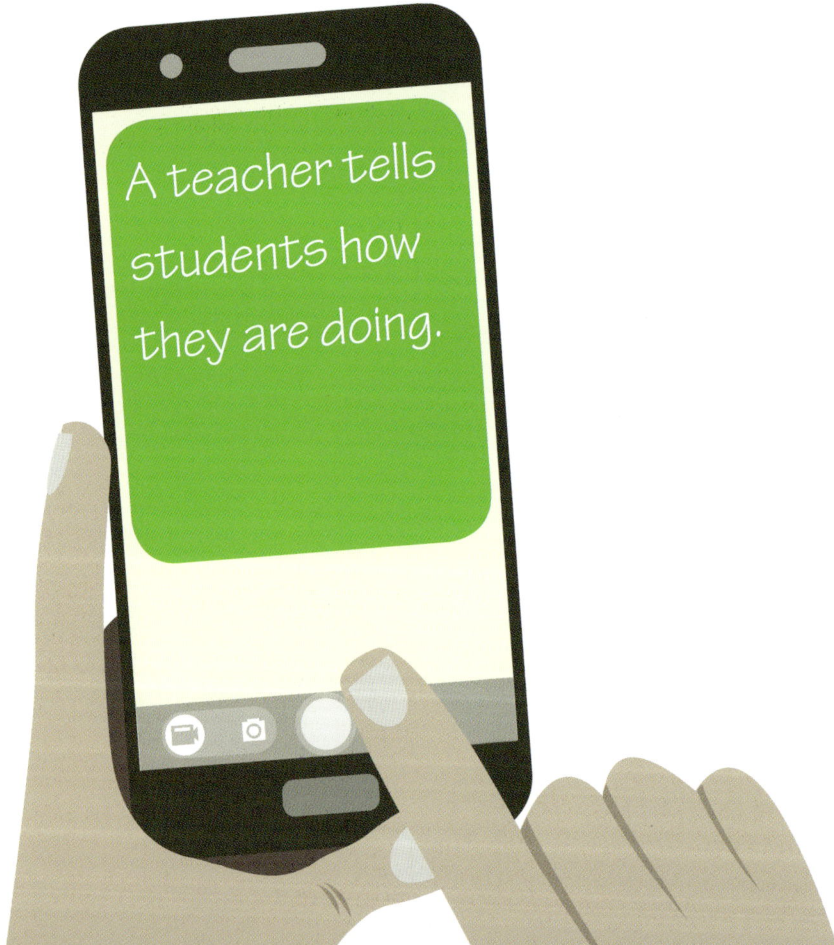

After School

It is the end of the day.

Teachers walk students to the bus.

Teachers meet after school.
They talk about helping students.

Teachers help kids learn and grow.

They are important to a community.

Activity

Interview with Your Teacher

An interview is when you ask someone questions. What would you like to ask your teacher?

Supplies
- paper
- pencil

Directions
1. Think about what questions you would like to ask. For example, "Why did you become a teacher?" could be a question.
2. Write three questions. Leave space below each question.
3. Ask your teacher these questions. Write each answer below the question.
4. Share your interview with a partner.

Photo Glossary

college (KAH-lij): A place for students to learn and study after they have finished high school.

lesson (LES-uhn): What students are taught during one time period at school.

model (MAH-duhl): To show how to do something.

principals (PRIN-suh-puhls): People who are in charge of schools.

Index

After Reading Activity

Pretend you are teaching someone how to make a sandwich. On a piece of paper, write the steps you would teach.

About the Author

Jeff Barger is an author, blogger, and literacy specialist. He lives in North Carolina. Jeff has been a teacher for 30 years. He has sharpened thousands of pencils.

www.rourkeeducationalmedia.com

Edited by: Kim Thompson
Cover and interior design by: Kathy Walsh

Photo Credits: Cover, title page, p.7, 20, 22: ©PeopleImages; p.5: ©Rawpixel.com; p.9: ©BraunS; p.11: ©monkeybusinessimages; p.13, 17, 22: ©Wavebreakmedia; p.15: ©Ridofranz; p.19, 22: ©Lokibaho

Library of Congress PCN Data

Teacher / Jeff Barger
(Community Helpers)
ISBN 978-1-73161-422-3 (hard cover)(alk. paper)
ISBN 978-1-73161-217-5 (soft cover)
ISBN 978-1-73161-527-5 (e-Book)
ISBN 978-1-73161-632-6 (ePub)
Library of Congress Control Number: 2019932039

Rourke Educational Media
Printed in the United States of America,
North Mankato, Minnesota